KU-779-886

Boa
and Breakfast

Michael and Joanne Cole

EGMONT

EGMONT

We bring stories to life

Original paperback edition first published in Great Britain 1977 by Methuen & Co. Ltd.
This edition first published in Great Britain 2016 by Egmont UK Limited,
The Yellow Building, 1 Nicholas Road, London W11 4AN
www.egmont.co.uk

Copyright © The Estate of Michael Cole 1977 and 2016
Endpaper and cover design by Lo Cole

ISBN 978 1 4052 8057 0

A CIP catalogue record for this title is available from the British Library.

All rights reserved. No part of this publication may be reproduced, stored in a retrieval system,
or transmitted, in any form or by any means, electronic, mechanical, photocopying, recording
or otherwise, without the prior permission of the publisher and copyright owner.

Stay safe online. Egmont is not responsible for content hosted by third parties.

MIX
Paper from
responsible sources
FSC® C018306

Bod is on his way to Barleymow's farm.
He has to step over a tree blown down
in the gale last night.

When Bod gets to the farm he sees Aunt Flo,
Frank the Postman and P.C. Copper walking
about the fields.

"Hello," says Bod. "What's up?"

Aunt Flo is behaving very strangely.
She is clucking and strutting about like a chicken.
"Why are you doing that?" asks Bod.

"Farmer Barleymow's chickens got out in the gale last night," says Aunt Flo. "If we pretend to be chickens they may come down from the trees to us."

The cows are out of their field, and Frank
the Postman is busy rounding them up.

"Delivering cows makes a change from delivering letters," says Frank.

P.C. Copper mounts the farm donkey
and rounds up the pigs and piglets.

"I've always wanted to be a mounted policeman," says P.C. Copper.

Bod, Aunt Flo, Frank and P.C. Copper
lead the animals back to the farm.

Farmer Barleymow finishes mending
all the fences, gates and doors that
have been blown down by the wind.

"You know, Barleymow," says P.C. Copper,
"I've never been over to your farm before."

"It would make an ideal spot
for a farmhouse holiday."

"Yes," says Aunt Flo,
"with your new-laid eggs . . .

. . . and fresh milk you could give
guests a wonderful bed and breakfast."

"Breakfast's no problem," says Barleymow.
"But what about the bed? There's only mine,
and I can't have all the guests in bed with me."

"I'll soon fix up the other bedrooms,"
says Frank. "Leave it to me."

"Children could have a lovely
holiday here too," says Bod.

"We could make a Pets' Corner
with all the baby animals."

"There's only one snag," says P.C. Copper.
"The farm's so tucked away people won't
be able to find it."

"I'll put up some signs. And I'll put up some cards in shop windows saying 'For Bed and Breakfast, Barleymow's best'."

When the house is ready, Bod and his friends leave Aunt Flo and Barleymow to prepare for the first guests.

"I wonder who they will be," says Barleymow.

The next day Frank arrives with a letter.

Barleymow opens the letter. It says
'Three gentlemen arriving tomorrow for bed and
breakfast – brown eggs please – and evening meal'.

"It's tomorrow today," says Aunt Flo, "because that letter was written yesterday. They may be here any minute. It's lucky I baked that pie!"

She is just taking the pie out of the oven when there's a knock at the door. "That must be them," she says. "I wonder who they are."
Barleymow goes to open the door.

"Hello," says Bod. "As it's so nice here we thought we'd be your first guests."
"Paying guests of course," says P.C. Copper.

"I wouldn't dream of you paying,"
says Barleymow. "Just be my guests.
Nothing would please me more!"

And so Barleymow provides the beds,
Aunt Flo makes the breakfasts, and they
all have a wonderful time helping on the farm.
"I must say," says Bod, "it's a very good idea this
Bod and Breakfast – Bed and Breakfast, I mean."